THREE'S A CROWD
and other family stories

Kate Blackadder

Published in 2016 by FeedARead.com Publishing

A CIP catalogue record for this title is available from the British Library.

These stories are works of fiction. They were first published in *The People's Friend* (in edited versions), *Woman's Weekly* and *Woman's Day* – see individual stories for details.

Contents

Class of '64   page 4

Hide-and-seek for Astronauts   11

In my Dreams   17

Celia's Surprise   20

'Are We Nearly There?'   25

The Generation Gap   32

The Night the Band Played   39

The New Eighteen   45

New Tricks, Old Tricks   49

Bicycles for Two   53

Seeing Natalie   62

Three's a Crowd   66

Class of '64

As she stood at the front door Emily could hear giggles coming from the sitting-room. Granny and her friend. The one they were going out with later to this reunion thing. Emily's heart sank at the thought of the evening ahead of her.

She let herself in, threw her schoolbag on the floor beside a huge suitcase, and stood in the sitting-room doorway.

Granny and a lady who must be her friend Kitty were wiping their eyes.

'The Prune! Her name was Prunella, wasn't it?' Granny put down her handkerchief.

'And do you remember Giraffe? Why did we call Miss Taylor that? She didn't have a particularly long neck, did she?'

Kitty went off in another gale of laughter.

'No, she didn't, but there was something giraffe-like about her posture. Remember when – ? Oh, hello there.'

'This is Emily,' Granny said. 'Darling, this is Kitty. We were in the same class in school, a long time ago.'

Kitty patted the space beside her on the sofa.

'Come and sit here, Emily. Aren't you lovely? She looks very like you, Marianne.'

Emily looked at her granny. Other people had said that but she couldn't see it herself.

'As your granny looked when I last saw her,' Kitty amended. 'All long legs and glossy red hair. I remember her school hat was always slipping off. I don't suppose you wear hats?'

'No, thank goodness,' Emily said, looking down at her short navy skirt, white blouse and green tie. 'School uniform's bad enough without a hat.'

'I think you look very stylish. Oh! Hats. That's what I was going to say about Giraffe – Giraffe was what we called our history teacher, Emily. Do you remember – ' Kitty

4

snorted, 'do you remember that time she called Slim Jim out for some misdemeanour or other, talking probably, and told him to stand behind the big blackboard?'

Apparently Granny remembered 'Slim Jim' too. 'And he found her cloche hat ... '

'And that ghastly fox fur she used to wear, with the glassy eyes ... '

'And put them on and peeked out from behind the board.' Granny reached for her hanky again.

'And when the class erupted he whisked behind it again so she never saw him. Three times he did that. And Giraffe had no idea what we were howling at. I thought I was going to burst.'

'Emily thinks we're about to burst now,' laughed Granny. 'Don't worry, darling, we'll go back to being sensible soon. After we left school, you see, Kitty emigrated to Canada with her family and we didn't see each other again until this afternoon. We have a lot to catch up on and we've started at the beginning.'

'My fault we never kept in touch. I was so homesick to start with I couldn't bear to think about life carrying on here without me. And then it seemed too late. I thought everyone would have forgotten me.' Kitty pulled down the corners of her mouth.

'I didn't forgot you,' Granny protested, 'but the magic thing is that fifty years have rolled away and we're all eighteen again.'

'But how did you find each other?' Emily asked.

'I joined Facebook,' said Kitty, 'and I saw that my old school had a page because they were planning a fifty-year reunion. Class of '64! I decided right away that I wanted to be there.'

'Granny! I said you should go on Facebook.' Emily grinned at Marianne.

'As you know I heard about the reunion anyway,' Granny smiled back. 'Another school friend told me about it in a very old-fashioned but useful thing called a phone call.'

5

Kitty laughed. 'I asked on Facebook if anyone knew anything about Marianne Kennedy as was, and someone gave me her number. And there she was, living a stone's throw from our old stamping-ground.'

'We moved away for a while,' Granny said, 'but we came back when our eldest was born.'

Kitty wagged her finger. 'Don't rush ahead. We haven't got to the husband yet. We're still in the classroom making life a misery for poor Miss Taylor. But I want to hear about Emily first. Do you go to the school we went to?'

'The Academy.' Emily nodded.

'It's not our old building,' Granny said. 'They built a new one years ago. Now, you two get to know each other. I'm going to make some tea.'

Why did it have to be this week that Dad went to Scotland on business and suggested Mum went with him for a little holiday? It meant Emily staying at Granny and Grandpa's – which usually she loved to do, but tonight they and Kitty were going to this reunion and Granny had gone and asked the organisers if Emily could go as well.

Great! So, instead of a cosy evening joking with Grandpa, watching TV, and scoffing Granny's home-made biscuits, she'd be at a party where everyone else would be almost seventy.

Kitty was peering short-sightedly at Granny and Grandpa's wedding photograph on the side table.

'I never had time to get married,' she said. 'Ran my own business, employment agencies all over Canada. Sold up last year. Think any of the guys there tonight will be looking for a rich wife?'

Was she serious? Emily laughed uncertainly. Kitty must be sixty-eight, the same age as Granny. Surely she was far too old to be looking for a 'guy'?

'Your granny was quite a girl, Emily.' Kitty glanced at the wedding photo again. 'Slim Jim, the boy who was always in trouble with Miss Taylor, he and Marianne were an item you know.' She sat down on the sofa again. 'One afternoon we skipped off school to see *Cleopatra* at the cinema. Marianne, Jim, me, and some lad, can't remember his name, real looker though. But Marianne and Jim took no notice of the film. They hid behind her panama hat getting in some kissing practice.'

'Kitty!' Granny hurried in, carrying a tray. Her face was bright pink. 'I could hear everything you said. I wouldn't have left you with Emily if I'd known you were going to be such a gossip!'

'Sorry,' Kitty said, sounding anything but. 'Marianne, what was the name of that lad, the one who looked like Richard Burton?'

'Alan Steel?'

'Alan Steel. Of course. I wonder if he'll be there tonight.' Kitty took the cup Marianne handed to her.

'I know for a fact he will be.' A smile tugged at the corners of Granny's mouth. 'I'm not sure about the Richard Burton resemblance though.'

'Well, we'll all have changed a little, I expect,' Kitty said.

Emily stuffed cake into her mouth to stop herself laughing. After fifty years everyone would have changed more than a little! Granny's hair, which Kitty said had once been red, was now silvery-gray. Kitty's own hair was blonde and she wore loads of make-up but there was no way she looked eighteen.

'So is Alan footloose and fancy free by any chance?' Kitty went on.

Granny shook her head. 'He has a very nice wife, five children and eleven grandchildren.'

'Goodness, he's been busy. Oh well.' Kitty cast a mischievous look at Emily. 'I daresay there will be some lonely hearts there for me to break. And what became of Slim Jim, do you know?'

Granny went pink again. 'That's him at the door now,' she said. 'He's been playing golf with Alan Steel.'

'You married Slim Jim?' Kitty threw up her hands and roared with laughter. 'Well, I never.'

7

Grandpa came in, his hands outstretched, his face alight with a welcoming smile. 'Kitty. You haven't changed a bit. Good to see you.'

'Good to see you too, Slim Jim.' Kitty stood up and kissed Grandpa on both cheeks. 'So, you married your childhood sweetheart?'

'And never regretted it.' Grandpa blew Granny a kiss. 'Oh, we're going to have a grand time tonight. And lovely to have our Emily with us too.'

Emily leapt up to hug him. His name should be Not-very-slim-Jim now! She tried to imagine him wearing a lady's hat and a horrible fox fur.

'So you'll be escorting three beautiful girls tonight, you lucky man,' said Kitty. 'Now, Marianne. Clothes. I've brought three outfits and I want you to help me decide on one.'

'I know what I'm wearing.' Grandpa winked at Emily. 'I'll leave you girls to it.'

'Emily came shopping with me last week,' Granny told Kitty. 'She's my fashion advisor these days. I got a lovely little black and white dress, and a new pair of red shoes. I've always loved red shoes.'

It had been a fun afternoon. Almost as good as going shopping with her friends, Emily thought. Granny tried on nine dresses before settling for this really smart one. Then she bought Emily a top as a thank you for helping her and they'd gone for hot chocolate.

'Sounds a knock-out,' Kitty said. She went through to the hall and came back dragging her suitcase which she proceeded to unbuckle and fling open.

She picked up a brightly patterned scarf and handed it to Marianne. 'Let's see if I've got something for Emily.' She rummaged further down and produced a round tin. 'Try these. Chocolatey. Nutty. They're gorgeous.' She rummaged some more and brought out a long silky blue dress, a knee-length black one with lace sleeves, and a leopard-print skirt, all of which she draped over the sofa before diving into the case again and coming up with a pair of shoes with very high heels and red soles.

'Wow,' said Emily, and Granny turned round from the mirror where she was admiring herself in her new scarf.

'Try them on if you like, both of you.' Kitty threw the shoes to Emily.

'Wow,' Emily said again, looking down at her feet. She couldn't move but the shoes looked a-m-a-z-i-n-g. She took them off and handed them to Granny who sashayed up and down the room in them with hardly a wobble.

Emily thought of the dress she planned to wear, now lying crumpled up in her schoolbag, and felt a little embarrassed. 'Can I borrow your iron, Granny?'

'Of course. You know where it is. Then will you help me with my make-up, darling? Kitty's putting me to shame in that department. Kit, I love that skirt. What would you wear with it?'

Emily went to retrieve her dress and almost jumped out of her skin. A man with long hair and little round spectacles was coming downstairs carrying a guitar.

He smiled at her and she realised it was Grandpa.

He flicked the hair off his forehead. 'How do I look?'

Surely Grandpa wasn't going out wearing a wig? Her question must have shown in her face.

Grandpa patted her arm. 'Don't worry. I won't put it on until we get there.'

'But why ... it's not as if you're totally bald.'

'Thank you, my pet. Some pals and I are doing a Beatles' tribute band spot tonight. Which one do you think I am?'

'Which what?'

'Which Beatle. John, Paul, George or Ringo?'

'I've heard of the Beatles. Weren't they famous back in the olden ... ' She stopped. 'I didn't know you could play the guitar.'

'And I bet you didn't know that your granny used to win twist competitions? You'll see her in action later. Now,' he said, strumming a chord on the guitar, 'I'm going to give the girls a surprise.' And 'Slim Jim' went off to clown around

9

just as he had done in Miss Taylor's classroom all those years ago.

What were twist competitions, Emily wondered, as she went to find the iron. Then, hearing the laughter explode in the sitting-room, she couldn't help laughing too. Imagine Grandpa playing in a band! And Kitty was great, really cool.

It was true what Granny had said. Everyone was eighteen tonight.

This was going to be a fun evening after all.

Published in *The People's Friend*

Hide-and-Seek for Astronauts

Last year, Julie hired a fire engine.

The year before, she had an igloo built in the garden – in June. The year before that she took ten four-year-olds on a steam train.

Now she had begun to talk about Ben's next birthday party although he wouldn't be seven for another two months. He was obsessed with space so I asked if she'd booked a supersonic trip around the galaxy with a stop for moon burgers.

'Very funny. Haven't finalised the details yet. Just keep the eighteenth free.'

When Julie and I were kids, our birthday parties were a few friends round to play in the garden and a home-made cake with candles half-burnt from their previous outing. I don't remember either of us ever getting new candles, but we didn't care.

'It's different now, Karen.' Julie was dismissive when I reminded her. 'Anyway, you don't have children.'

I may not have children of my own but as an infant teacher I see more than enough of them. Julie was right. It is different now. We thought that life didn't get any better than playing hide-and-seek and looking forward to a big piece of Gran's jammy sponge. But that all came free, more or less – now birthday parties seemed to be about spending money and not just keeping up with the Joneses but leap-frogging over them.

Julie had become an expert leap-frogger, and spending money was one of her favourite occupations. As was trying to persuade me to spend my hard-earned.

'Why don't we go shopping for some new clothes for you?' she asked me. We were sitting having a Saturday morning cappuccino. It was just ten o'clock but she was carrying several shiny carrier bags from one of the designer shops in the precinct.

'What for? They'll just get poster paint and sticky finger marks all over them.'

'You don't teach all the time. Matthew suggested … '

'Matthew suggested what?'

'Nothing.'

'Julie.' I gave her the look I give P1 when they're particularly fractious and she capitulated.

'We were watching one of those makeover programmes and he said why didn't I put you forward?'

'As if! I'm not going to parade in my underwear, or worse, for all the world to see. What would Gran have said?'

What Gran would have said to such an event was beyond our imagination, and we dissolved into giggles.

'I can't see you doing it,' Julie conceded. 'But you could do with a new look.'

I wasn't offended. Julie meant well and we had this conversation, or variations on it, regularly.

'I really can't be bothered,' I said. 'You do the glam bit for both of us.'

To be fair, I knew that Julie would be happy to pass her cast-offs on to me and I would have been happy to take them. It was unfortunate that I, the older sister whose hand-me-downs Julie was forced to wear as a child, was three inches shorter than her and a completely different shape.

Julie was still thinking about Gran.

'We hardly had any clothes that weren't second-hand or home-made,' she went on. 'Remember the paper pattern she kept making those pinafore dresses from? The same one she'd used for our mum. And those scratchy jumpers?' She pulled a face.

I didn't tell her that I still had the moss green chunky polo neck Gran knitted for me when I was fourteen, and that I wore it on winter nights when I got in from school.

'She tried to teach us to sew and knit but that was a lost cause.' Julie finished her coffee and patted her red lips with a napkin. 'Sure you don't want me to come shopping with you?'

I was sure.

But when I was getting ready for bed, Matthew's suggestion came back to me. I looked at the nubbly tweed skirt I'd just flung on the chair. I'd had it for five years but it was still perfectly serviceable. The top I was taking off was in a shade of blue I didn't particularly like but it had been on a half-price rail.

I didn't envy Julie her designer lifestyle. Fun for a day maybe but what a palaver. Sometimes I wondered what Gran, with her one ancient lipstick and her three-times-a-year perm, would think of Julie's manicures and facials and whatnots, not to mention her built-in wardrobes and her forests of shoe-trees.

The nubbly skirt went on again on Monday with a top, mustard this time, from the same sale rail. Even I could see that the colour didn't suit me; the face that stared back at me looked to be the last stages of yellow fever.

Maybe I should make more of an effort.

Everything seemed to go wrong that morning. When I was gulping down some cereal my cat, Scatty, jumped on the table and knocked over the milk carton. The traffic, even in the bus lane, was worse than usual. P1 was playing up and my fiercest looks did nothing to quell them.

And when I had a break in the staff room at lunch-time there came a hysterical call on my mobile from Julie saying she was at the school gate and did I have a minute.

I hurried outside.

'Matthew's been made redundant. His whole department. As of now. Told to clear their desks. Karen, he's crying.'

She burst out crying herself.

I hugged her, looking at my watch over her shoulder. 'I've got eight minutes. Come and sit down.' There was a bus shelter just along the road and luckily we had it to ourselves.

'I just had to get out of the house for a little while. I don't know what to say to Matthew. He's gone to pieces. He keeps going on about all the extra hours he worked, all the weekends he went into the office. Time he could have spent with Ben and me. And this is the thanks he gets.'

I kept my arm around her and let her talk.

Eventually she wiped her eyes and stood up. 'You've got to get back. And Matthew and I have to pull ourselves together before Ben gets home.'

'Shall I come round tonight or do you want to be on your own?'

'No. Please come. Thanks, Karen.'

I found it hard to concentrate on P1's reading skills, or lack of them, that afternoon. Of course, Julie hadn't married Matthew just for his potential earning power, but part of the attraction definitely was that their future children would have all the things that she didn't have growing up – new clothes, music lessons, foreign holidays. Themed birthday parties. And nothing home-made.

Then, as Matthew got further and further up the corporate ladder and the future children started, and stopped, with Ben, she had the time and money to reinvent herself as an immaculate, high-maintenance clothes-horse.

Now that Matthew, with the fickle fall of economic dice, had fallen into the snake-pit of unemployment how would Julie cope?

When she opened the door to me that night she looked as immaculate as ever apart from a little pinkness around the nose.

But in the kitchen as I helped her load the dishwasher her eyes welled up again.

'Matthew says we can't go on holiday this year. And Ben can't have all the birthday surprises I was planning. And – '

Despite the money lavished on him, Ben's unspoilt, a great kid and I love him to bits. 'Ben won't mind. Look how thrilled he was that Matthew can pick him up from school tomorrow. It's people that matter to children, not things.'

She didn't look convinced.

We developed a code over the next few weeks. I never asked in words if Matthew had any job prospects. I would raise my eyebrows and Julie would shake her head and then we'd talk about something else.

We stopped having coffee in the shopping centre. She came to me one week and I went to her the next.

As the eighteenth of June approached, Julie was fretting over Ben's birthday party.

'I had all these great ideas but now we have to economise I don't know what to do.' She picked up a chocolate digestive and put it down again.

I resisted an elder sisterly urge to slap her.

'You don't need to spend loads of money to have a good time. Get a grip, Julie. We were happy with Gran and Gramps weren't we? Even though they didn't have two pennies to rub together?'

'I hated never having anything new.'

'They did their best. Imagine them, just about to retire and then losing their daughter and being landed with a four-year-old and a baby to look after.'

'I know, I know. But,' she fell back on her favourite excuse, 'it's different now.'

I looked around Julie's lounge. There were sliding doors into the dining area. With these open, the floor area would be even bigger. Big enough for a dozen seven-year-olds …

In the event, the eighteenth of June was a perfect summer's day and Ben and his fellow astronauts played hide-and-seek in the garden before coming into the spaceship for moon burgers.

Julie's lounge curtains were drawn and the central light glowed eerily under a blue and mustard-yellow patchwork shade. At intervals, suspended from the ceiling on lengths of thread, were the planets – round cushions of nubbly tweed covered in silver foil. It all looked great, though we said so ourselves, and had been surprisingly good fun to put together.

The astronauts looked suitably impressed for about thirty seconds before stampeding to the table.

In pride of place was a home-made cake shaped like a rocket. Seven whole candles formed a ring of fire on the launch pad.

As Julie and I were sampling the cake – it was scrumptious – I remembered I hadn't asked my usual question.

I raised my eyebrows at Julie and this time she didn't shake her head.

Then she did.

'Matthew hasn't got a job. Although he's muttering about taking up baking professionally. But I have.' She grinned at the look on my face. 'In my favourite shop in the precinct. Personal shopper with management prospects.'

'That's amazing.' I stuffed the last bit of cake into my mouth and hugged her.

'I can get you a discount,' she said. 'As you've just cut up half your wardrobe.'

I took a deep breath. 'I would appreciate your expert advice.' I grinned at her. 'When they've got a sale on.'

I was just about to ask what she thought about taking dressmaking classes when we had to rush to the table to stop two of the astronauts going completely into orbit.

Actually, some things aren't so different now.

Children are just as noisy and messy as they've always been. And the secret of a successful birthday party is still a game of hide-and-seek, and a big piece of jammy sponge.

Published in *Woman's Weekly*

In my dreams

Yes, I know it's just a dream but I'm going to enjoy it while I can. I've got a lot on my mind I'll be glad to forget for a while. Besides, it's not every night that Brad Pitt pops in for a cuppa.

And it's not everyone who remembers their dreams. I always do, and on top of that, according to an article I read, I'm an advanced dreamer. I know when I'm dreaming and I can decide, say, to parachute jump, confident that I'll land safely. Or I can go off into the sunset, if you know what I mean, with Colin Firth, well, Mr Darcy, knowing I'll wake up next to my husband with a clear conscience, knowing nothing has really happened. Mr Darcy gets a regular guest spot in the world I inhabit after I've gone to sleep.

Brad's never appeared before, but it's nice to see him anyway, making himself at home in this kitchen. It's not my kitchen though. It has a bright pink American fridge, the exact pink of the t-shirt I'll be wearing tomorrow. Brad explains why he's here. He met my sister apparently and she told him to look us up when he was in England.

Funny. I spoke to Izzy on skype this evening, our time, and she never mentioned him! But then she had a difficult afternoon ahead of her. Oh, wait a minute. When I nipped out to the corner shop for eggs and passed the stand of gossipy magazines by the door, I saw Brad on the cover of one because he's broken up with Angelina, and on another saying he and Angelina want six more children. So that's why he was in my sub-conscious, why he's turned up tonight. If the opportunity presents itself I'll ask him if either of these stories are true.

I've made a pot of tea – Brad's happy with English Breakfast – and I'm sitting snipping recipes out of a magazine and listening to Brad and my ten-year-old son talking about films. Actually, my son seems to be doing most of the talking, about a film he'd like to make and which he wonders if Brad might invest in. The film will need lots of special effects. It will star, of course, himself, and his friend next door, and they're looking for someone to play the alien who's taken over their tree-house. Perhaps Brad ... ? I try to kick my son under the table but even an advanced dreamer doesn't always manage that.

It turns out though that this dream isn't really about Brad. Someone else is about to come on stage.

Probably to avoid handing over some of his hard-earned time and money to the Back Garden Production Company – although in my opinion he's missing a trick – Brad announces that his dog is in the car, and it's sick, he's really worried about it. We insist that he brings it into the house and he goes out and returns with an adorable golden retriever puppy who does indeed look a little under the weather. My son says he has a hang-dog expression.

But the dream is not about a golden retriever pup either, however adorable.

My mother comes in and says she will take the dog to the vet.

The world shrinks, like a film close-up, to Mum's face, her soft brown eyes and the little worry lines between her brows. Keeping her in my sight I walk shakily towards her. 'Mum? Mum, I thought you were ... dead.'

Mum smiles, but offers no explanation as to how this misunderstanding can have arisen. She's wearing a dress I remember cutting up for patches years ago, a round-necked, full-skirted dress, glazed cotton, purple flowers and green leaves on a white background.

I'm terrified I'll wake up before I reach her, but I get there and she's solid flesh under my arms as I hug her and hug her and cry and cry ...

The tears are there, running down my face when the alarm clock breaks up our reunion.

But the kitchen and the pink fridge have disappeared. So have Brad and his puppy. My son is eighteen, gone away to university. And Mum has gone. I'm in bed, fumbling in the dark to silence the ringing, while trying to will myself back to dreamland for one more hug.

Then I realise it's not the clock that's wakened me. The mobile phone on my bedside table is lit up.

Izzy.

It's been difficult getting used to the time difference since she moved to San Francisco but I told her to ring the minute she heard, whatever time it was here. I pick up the phone as I climb out of bed, quietly so as not to disturb my husband, and pad through to the kitchen with fear in my heart.

Izzy tells me that it's good news, that the lump was benign, that the doctor says there's nothing to worry about.

New tears come, mine and hers, but then we get a grip and Izzy says it must be one o' clock with you, were you asleep? I tell her about my dream. Just the Brad bit – we've had enough emotion for one night. She laughs and promises she'll send him our way if the occasion arises.

We linger, not wanting to break the connection.

'I was thinking about Mum,' Izzy says softly. 'How brave she was when her news was different from mine.'

'I'll be thinking of you both tomorrow,' I say and she wishes me luck before we hang up.

Pirate, the 57-varieties rescue dog we got to fill our empty nest, is in his basket in the hall. He doesn't open his eyes but his tail wags slightly. I wonder what he's dreaming about.

I slide back into bed and think about tomorrow's charity run. I'll wear my bright pink t-shirt and, in my dreams, Mum and Izzy will be there to cheer me on.

Published in *Woman's Weekly*

Celia's Surprise

'Jennifer, it's almost eleven o'clock,' Simon calls upstairs.

'Just coming.'

I'm not used to wearing a hat. I adjust it in front of the mirror again. We have plenty of time but Simon makes Big Ben look tardy.

He's waiting by the door, jingling his keys. He looks me up and down. Knee length pale green and white dress, emerald green shoes and little emerald green hat. Simon doesn't say anything but he smiles and raises his eyebrows and I know him well enough to take that as a compliment.

'You're looking pretty good yourself,' I say, flicking a piece of fluff from the lapel of his suit, the one he wore when we got married.

'Have you any idea what Celia will be wearing? Not her usual I hope,' he says, sliding the car smoothly into gear.

'She told me she was going shopping with someone, that's all I know.'

He snorts. No doubt he is thinking of Celia's usual attire of long patchwork skirts, baggy velvet tops and armfuls of bangles. Simon has a horror of anything that could be described as bohemian. According to him, he had a ghastly childhood being teased because his real name is Sylvan. The first thing he did when he was eighteen was to change it by deed poll.

And no doubt he is thinking too of Celia's friends and whether any of them could be relied on to help her chose a suitable outfit.

'She's made a lot of friends over the last four years,' I muse.

We've met some of them at Celia's various parties. She loves to throw parties.

'I hope she didn't mean that Eliot whatshisname she had in tow the last time we saw her,' Simon growls.

'Eliot was lovely,' I protest, 'really interesting, and anxious to be friendly.'

'Too anxious.' Simon loosens up suddenly and turns to grin at me. 'Oh well, she's old enough to choose her own friends, live her own life. But it is her graduation. I hope she makes some effort. Where did she say we were to meet her?' he asks.

It's a typical Celia arrangement.

If we're there by quarter to twelve she might be outside the hall but we're only to wait for five minutes and if she's doesn't appear we're to go in and sit down. She'll see us in the foyer afterwards and we'll go out for lunch.

I remind Simon of all this. He tenses up again, wrinkling his nose.

'I hope we're not going to that awful bean place she took us to before. Full of students. The place with the sticky forks and no napkins.' He shudders.

'She is a student,' I say, 'but I've booked a table at *La Maison Rouge*, for four in case she wants to bring anybody.'

'Good. At least we'll get a decent meal.'

He subsides and concentrates on the new one-way system, then frowns as we join what seems to be a long queue of stationary cars. It's some time before we move up and Simon keeps checking his watch, drumming his fingers on the steering wheel.

By the time we've found a parking space it's exactly quarter to twelve

Predictably, Celia is nowhere to be seen but suddenly Eliot is there in front of us, a stocky, smiling figure. He's had his beard and hair trimmed since we saw him last and his golden brown corduroy suit looks new. He shakes Simon's hand, turns to shake mine, changes his mind and throws his arms round me. It's like being hugged by a big friendly teddy bear.

'Let's go in,' he says. 'Celia's sitting with her classmates.'

'Thank you, Eliot,' I say, since Simon does not reply.

21

Eliot has evidently been in the hall earlier and bagged three seats, good seats near the front. One of the privileges of being a Professor, I suppose. He leans forward and looks at us, his hazel eyes alight with mischief.

'Celia has a bit of a surprise for you. Look, she's coming in now.'

We turn as a crowd of students comes down the aisle. Celia sees us and waggles her fingers. She is walking tall and proud, her black gown flowing out behind her, but it's what else she's wearing that makes Simon and I gasp.

Her skirt is long but it is black and elegant. Her top is deep red velvet but is fitted and has no embroidery or sparkly bits. She's not wearing any bangles as far as I can see. She is wearing shoes, not sandals. Most transforming of all is her thick dark hair, up in a neat chignon rather than hanging loose.

But that isn't the surprise.

We watch a seemingly endless procession of graduates go up to the stage. They go in alphabetical order so Celia is nearly the last. I'm so absorbed in watching her stand up as her name is called that it is only when she is on the stage that I realise what the Dean has said.

Celia Margaret Walker, archaeology, first class.

Eliot is beaming from ear to ear. Simon's mouth is hanging open. I expect mine is too.

A first-class degree. She never told us. Just phoned and said she'd passed and she hoped we would come to the graduation.

Simon had treated it as a joke, Celia going to university. She's always had terrific enthusiasms, things she started but didn't see through. Making jewellery, being a Mediterranean tour guide, doing a computer course, floristry – every time we saw her she seemed to be doing something different. Then it was volunteering at a local dig for Roman remains and the announcement that she wanted to study archaeology. Not with the Open University – she wanted the whole student experience. What she said in her application and at her interview we'll never know but she was accepted by one

22

of the top courses in the country. She'll never stick it, Simon kept saying, but one year turned into two, then three and four.

We sit, dazed, through the rest of the Ws, a Y and a Z. Then it's all over and Eliot is ushering us through the throng to the foyer where Celia is waiting.

When she has extricated herself from one of Eliot's hugs, Celia looks at us. She seems uncharacteristically unsure of herself.

'Simon! What do you think of your old mum then?' she asks, patting her hair.

'Why didn't you tell us, Celia? You've done so well. A first-class degree! That's terrific,' I say.

'Thank you, Jennifer darling,' says Celia, but her eyes are still on Simon.

My husband does not find it easy to express his feelings. He was brought up in some sort of commune in California, a time he refuses to talk about now. Neither Celia nor he has seen his father since they came back to England when he was seven, when he started to turn himself from a curly-haired wild child (Celia's showed me the photographs) into the short-back-and-sides lawyer I fell in love with.

Celia, on the other hand, never got over her hippy phase and has teased her son over the years for being grey-suited and straight-laced and punctual and tidy. But now it seems that she's anxious for his approval.

Simon clears his throat. He opens his mouth but nothing comes out.

'Oh for goodness sake.' Celia moves forward and holds out her arms and my twenty-eight-year-old husband steps into them like a little boy.

Eliot puts his hand under my elbow, steers me aside, and makes small talk for five minutes.

Then they join us, Celia's arm linked through Simon's.

'Has Eliot been telling you our news?' she asks me brightly.

'No, my love, I've left that for you,' Eliot says, smiling.

It seems that Celia is full of surprises today. 'Well. Eliot's taking a sabbatical and we're going to Turkey for a year. Some fabulous ancient glass has been found in one of the sites there and that's Eliot's thing. He's going to write a book about it. And I've got a research grant to go and help. I can't wait – it all sounds *fascinating*.'

'And?' prompts Eliot gently.

'Oh, yes.' If this weren't Celia I would swear she was blushing. 'We thought we might get married. You know me, try anything once.'

Simon's eyes meet mine.

Surely he's not deceived by Celia's flippancy. Don't spoil it, I beg him silently. Say the right thing.

He clears his throat.

The three of us look at him anxiously.

He opens his mouth.

'That's something else first-class to celebrate,' he says, and there's a collective sigh of relief. 'Jennifer's booked a table at *La Maison Rouge* for one-forty-five.' He looks at his watch. 'We better not be …'

He stops. He loosens the knot of his tie.

He takes a deep breath, turns to Celia and says bravely:

'Unless you'd rather go to that bean place.'

Published in *Woman's Day* (Australia) under the title *A Class Act*

'Are We Nearly There?'

'Mum! Don't! Someone might hear you!'

I stopped singing along with the CD, turned the volume down and looked at Abby in the rear view mirror. 'Like who, my pet? The sheep?'

Abby made a face. 'Just don't expect me to listen.'

She stuck her earphones firmly in and lay back with her eyes shut, her little dog, Dot, cuddled beside her. His eyes were shut too but one ear was flipped up. Maybe he didn't like my singing any more than my daughter did.

When I was eight, Abby's age, I passed the time on car journeys sucking barley sugar and fighting with my brother. And, of course, endlessly asking the question Abby asked now without opening her eyes.

'Are we nearly there?'

I crossed my fingers as much as the steering wheel would allow. 'Not very long now.'

Which wasn't true, I'm afraid. We'd been on the road early but it would be eleven before we reached the ferry terminal, the boat would take almost two hours, plus we'd have a car journey at the other end.

'We'll stop soon to stretch our legs. Then we'll have lunch on the boat,' I said. 'Daddy said they had very good soup. He had his up on deck, like a picnic!'

Abby wasn't impressed. 'I won't feel like eating anything. Actually, I'll probably be sick.'

I turned the volume up again. Last week I was thrilled when I spotted a CD of Scottish songs in the supermarket, perfect for the journey north. When the last track ended I pressed the replay button, glancing in the mirror. Abby was leaning against a heap of stuff taking up the other half of the back seat and appeared to be asleep. I didn't wake her up to tell her that we were just crossing the border into Scotland.

It seemed a very long time since I went camping in the Highlands with some friends and met Peter who turned out to be from my home town. After we got married we always intended to go back up for a holiday, but somehow it never happened. Then Peter's dream job came up – on an island off the west coast of Scotland. Abby had never been further north than Newcastle, nor been on a boat bigger than a rowing boat in the park. And neither Peter nor I had lived on an island before. That would be a new experience for all of us.

He went on ahead three months ago leaving me to sell our house, and Abby to finish the school term. We'd both missed him a lot.

I stopped in a lay-by at the edge of a moor and opened my door quietly. The ground was damp with recent rain and the air was fresh and cool. I opened Abby's door, leaned in and removed her earphones. She didn't move. I lifted Dot out and put on his lead. I didn't want him rushing away in excitement and getting lost.

He got excited anyway at all the new smells and ran this way and that. As he sniffed I looked at the tiny flowers and the grasses, and the heather just about to come into colour, until I realised my shoes were getting muddy and I pulled a reluctant little dog back to the car.

Abby opened her eyes. 'Is this Scotland?' she asked sleepily. 'I don't like the look of it.'

I could see from her perspective that the great expanse of moorland was not the most exciting sight in the world. Nor would she be very interested to hear about its vegetation.

'Dot likes it,' I said. 'Have a little run round then you can open the sweeties Granny gave you.'

When she came back she asked if she could sit in the front seat.

'I don't see why not,' I said, heaving a box from the front to the back to make room.

Abby opened the glove compartment, took out a packet of photos Peter had sent from the island and shuffled through them.

'Why do we have to move there?' she asked for the hundredth time.

'Daddy's got a job there as a nature warden, looking after the birds and animals and telling people about them,' I replied. For the hundredth time. 'Just what he's always wanted to do. It will be an adventure. And you'll make lots of new friends. Everybody knows everybody on an island.'

Abby peered at the picture of our new home, a white cottage with green painted window frames and front door, and a fence round it to keep the sheep out of the garden. 'It's really small. Granny said it looks as if it has no electricity or bathroom.'

My mother was less than enthusiastic about our moving so far away.

'Of course it's got electricity, and a bathroom,' I said. 'Later on, when we're all unpacked and sorted out, Granny can come up and see for herself. Besides, it's bigger than it looks in that picture. There's an extension out the back. You can have the bedroom looking on to the beach.'

'Can Dot sleep on my bed? He'll be nervous in a new place.'

I thought that if having Dot on her bed would help Abby herself to settle I would have no objection, but for the moment I fell back on that favourite phrase of mothers everywhere.

'We'll see,' I said. 'The map that Dad made for you is in there with the photos. Do you want to see it?'

Peter had sent Abby a map he'd drawn of the island showing special things he thought she'd like – an ice-cream shop, a field of Highland cows, her new school, a shell beach, a ruined castle.

'Look, Abby, that's our new house. It's called Seal View,' I'd pointed out.

'That's a stupid name.'

She wouldn't look at the map then and she wouldn't look at it now.

As I started the car she extracted a picture of Peter, apparently taken by one of our new neighbours, standing at the cottage door. She laid it on the dashboard.

'Now it's like Daddy is in the car with us.'

'I'm dreading the drive,' I'd confessed to Peter when he phoned the night before. 'You know what it's like, even the shortest journey seems to Abby to take forever. And she's still worried at the thought of changing schools and everything.'

'She'll love it when she's here,' Peter said optimistically. 'Don't say anything in case I can't make it but I'm hoping to be able to come and meet you off the boat.'

Abby looked out of the window as we passed lochs and villages. 'We're passed that boring bit now,' she said. 'Are we nearly … ?'

'Look,' I said quickly, 'over there. Can you see the sea?'

'I've never been out in the middle of the sea before,' Abby said. 'Granny thinks the water will be very wild and the boat will roll around.'

I wished my mother would keep her thoughts to herself. 'Well, some days it might,' I said, 'but probably not in July.'

Once again I crossed my fingers, as I looked up at the darkening sky.

We joined the queue of cars waiting for the ferry. I had anticipated that Abby might get bored with the wait so I produced a new book to read aloud, about a pirate and his parrot. It kept us fully occupied until we moved forward to be expertly guided into the bowels of the ferry.

'Don't forget Dot's lead,' I said to Abby. 'And I think we better take our rain jackets with us.'

Abby carried Dot up the narrow steps. We looked at all the people sitting in rows and caught the smell of chips, sharp and cloying at the same time, and carried on till we were right on the top deck. Our backs were to the town and the ferry and we seemed to be surrounded by sea.

Unexpectedly, Abby seemed thrilled. 'I'll pretend I'm a pirate,' she said, 'and Dot is my parrot.'

'I don't think he'll be very happy sitting on your shoulder,' I said and we both giggled.

We found what seemed to be a sheltered spot. I took out the book again and Abby leaned against me, her faithful 'parrot' sleeping on her feet. I carried on reading until the wind whipping the pages made it impossible.

'Do you want to go downstairs?' I asked Abby.

She shook her head. 'I like it here,' she said, her hair blowing across her face.

'Well, put your fleece on. And your waterproof on top,' I added as big drops of rain began to fall.

She bent over and tickled Dot behind the ears.

'Let's go for a walk with my parrot.' We held onto each other and onto Dot and walked all the way round the deck. Everyone else had retreated below. We wiped the rain from our faces, leaned over the rail and watched the white furrows made by the boat ploughing through the dark blue sea.

Abby was humming quietly to herself. *Speed bonnie boat like a bird on the wing.* She must have been listening to my CD after all.

'You'll have to write and tell Granny that you love it when the water is wild,' I teased.

'I'm starving now.' Abby tugged at my arm. 'Please can we get something to eat? Try the soup that Daddy had?'

We bought filled rolls and brought them up on deck, together with cardboard cartons of soup. It was green split pea, thick and hot and savoury. I thought Abby might not like it but she finished hers first.

'That was yummy.' She wiped her fingers and went to put her rubbish in the bin. Then she lifted Dot, tucked him tightly under her arm, and looked out over the water. She made a circle with the index finger and thumb of her other hand and squinted through it.

'Mum! Land ahoy!' she shouted, as the island hills and the harbour came closer and closer.

And there was Peter, the first person we saw when the car rolled off the ferry.

'Daddy!' Abby tugged at the door handle.

'Abby! Wait until I can pull over.'

When I found a space to stop without causing a pile-up Abby was out of the car in a trice and in her father's arms, telling him about our journey and asking him questions in one breathless jumble.

I slid over to let Peter into the driving seat.

Abby leaned forward and put her chin on her father's shoulder.

'How far do we have to go, Dad?'

'You remember on the map I sent you? First of all we come to a ...'

'I haven't looked at it yet,' said Abby in a small voice.

I took it out of the glove compartment and held it up to show her. 'Here we are, just leaving the ferry port. So we're going from here,' I measured the distance with my fingers, 'to our house, here.'

Abby took the map from me and peered at it. 'It says Seal View! And there's a picture of a baby seal!'

'Yes, I told you that's what the house is called.'

'I thought you said *Sea* View. Will there really be seals? Have you seen any, Dad? Have you?'

'Had breakfast with one this morning,' Peter said, winking at her in the rear view mirror.

Abby bounced with excitement. She followed every millimetre of the map as we passed the ice cream shop, the cows, the school, the shell beach, giving Dot a running commentary.

'Now, we've just passed the ruined castle,' she said importantly, 'you must turn left here, Dad. This is the road to our very own house.'

Peter and I exchanged smiles as he slowed down and turned left.

'Road' turned out to be a bit of an exaggeration. We bumped along for a few hundred yards.

The rain had stopped. Peter turned off the windscreen wipers and cut the engine.

'What do you think, girls?' he asked.

Abby and I saw Seal View at the top of a short slope, a small white house with green painted woodwork, just as it was in the photograph. There was a fence round it, just as there was in the photograph. What hadn't been in the

30

photograph though was a banner tied onto the green gate. Abby unbuckled her seat belt and leaned forward in between us to see it better.

She read aloud the big black letters, splodged with rain but still legible:

WELCOME ABBY.
YOU'RE NEARLY THERE!

Published in *The People's Friend* under the title *The Long and Winding Road*

The Generation Gap

'Your great-great-grandfather was an engineer and inventor, you know,' I said to Gabriella who responded in the usual way by rolling her eyes.

I ploughed on. 'I think you take after him. You're practical and good at problem-solving, and at drawing.'

She yawned.

My daily resolution not to fall out with my infuriating fourteen-year-old daughter snapped before eleven o' clock in the morning.

'Gabriella. You have to choose your subjects by tomorrow. Can you stop painting your nails while I'm talking to you? We have to leave in five minutes and I'd rather have this conversation now than leave it till this evening.'

'Mum. I don't want to talk about it any time.' She condescended to put the polish bottle down.

'But it's important. Decisions you make now affect the rest of your life.' Ridiculous but true. 'You have to take English and maths and a science and … '

'I'll sort it out.' She sighed. 'I wish it was still the days when you could leave when you were fourteen.'

'You don't mean that.'

'I do. It's boring and … '

'What are you two arguing about now?' asked my husband, sticking his head round the door. 'Are you ready? I want to leave before the roads get busy.'

'Just coming. Come on, Gabriella. I only hope your granny can talk some sense into you.'

She didn't reply but huddled into her i-pod as she got into the back of the car.

Of course, she was all smiles and hugs for her grandparents when we arrived for our monthly Sunday lunch and even disappeared with her father and grandfather to do the washing up afterwards.

I told my mother about my 'discussion' with Gabriella earlier.

'You're very alike, you and your daughter,' Mum said, and I expostulated that, in comparison, I had been a very easy teenager.

'Well, you turned into a lovely thirty-something, darling.' Mum stood up. 'Why don't I get Christina's memoir to show her? This might be a good moment.'

Christina was my great-grandmother. She was born on a Hebridean island and came to Edinburgh in the mid 1880s, when she was eighteen, to work in service.

After her death, her son – my grandfather – found in her desk what appeared to be a memoir. Unfortunately, mice had got into the drawer and most of the paper had been chewed, but he carefully preserved the one readable page and in due course it was handed down to my mother who kept it between the leaves of a large dictionary.

'Come over to the table, dear,' my mother said now to Gabriella who obeyed her immediately without a sulk or a frown in sight.

Mum opened the book.

'This was written by my own granny, over a hundred years ago, when she wasn't much older than you. When you've read that side turn it over very gently.'

Gabriella leant over the paper, her face screwed up in concentration.

I remembered the first time I saw it myself. Christina's personality came shining through her beautiful copperplate handwriting and I so wished I'd known her.

'Are ye lost, lassie?'

The words were kind, and the woman looked elderly, but she gripped my wrist with a surprisingly strong hand.

I was lost. My mistress had sent me out from her grand house in the Royal Mile to buy skeins of embroidery silks. She'd drawn me a map, so pretty with its place names and coloured lines, but I couldn't read it. I had no idea which street I was in but I didn't want to say so. I didn't trust this cailleach *with one eye looking at her nose and the other over her shoulder, poor creature though she was.*

Gabriella snorted with laughter. She pointed to the paper. 'What does that word mean?'

'Cailleach?' said my mother. 'It's Gaelic for old lady.' She narrowed her eyes in amusement at Gabriella. 'Don't you be calling me that, miss!'

'I won't, Granny.' Gabriella smiled back at her. 'Look, this must be another Gaelic word, mach mach … I wonder how do you pronounce it?'

Machamarathad *I said, which, if you know the Gaelic, is not very polite, and I tried to pull my arm away. She held on and we swayed to and fro until she suddenly let go and I stumbled backwards, then she was off at a speed faster than I would have anticipated. I realised that the cloth purse with the money my mistress had given me was no longer attached to my waist. I gave chase but a young man was also in pursuit and he retrieved the purse.*

That was how I met James.

There was certainly no one like him back home on the Isle of Barra. He had to come and be inspected by Lady Stewart-Baillie before she allowed me to see him once a month on my afternoon off. He was very polite and tidily dressed in his Sunday best that day, and my Lady gave her permission.

But when we met every fourth Friday after that his hair was all over the place and his clothes were spattered with stains and scorch marks from his experiments.

As we strolled around Holyrood Park he told me his latest ideas. He took crumpled pieces of paper from his pocket and showed me drawings of strange machines and gadgets that he intended to have manufactured one day. I wish I could live for another hundred years, Christina, he said. Then there will be engines that can land on the moon, ships that can fly around the world – even a machine to wash your Lady's clothes so there will be no need for servants.

The way he spoke, I wanted it all to be true but of course I didn't believe a word of it – a machine to wash clothes!

'What did they do before washing machines?' asked my twenty-first-century daughter.

My mother mimed washing clothes by hand. Gabriella pulled a face and continued reading.

I told my Lady all about it when I got back – she always asked me if I'd had a pleasant afternoon. We didn't have grand ladies on Barra so I had no experience of them, but Annie the parlour-maid said Lady Stewart-Baillie was considered shocking in some quarters because she spoke to her servants as if they were as good as herself!

She expressed great interest in James's machines and put many questions to me about them that I was unable to answer but promised I would ask James to explain.

She looked in her desk for a piece of paper.

'I'm going to tell you something, Christina, something disgraceful. Two years ago, in this very city, a minister preached a sermon when he said' – she looked at the paper and read out – ''to educate young women like young men is a thing inexpedient and immodest'.'

She held the paper out to me.

'Read it for yourself, Christina. Inexpedient and immodest!'

I looked at the paper and then at my Lady.

'Disgraceful,' I agreed. 'I have heard ministers on the Isle of Barra say much the same. It's why, my Lady, I'm not able to read your paper.'

Gabriella gasped. 'They didn't want girls to go to school?'

Mum nodded. 'That's right. Unbelievable, isn't it? Read on, darling.'

This time Gabriella read aloud.

So that was when she started to give me lessons in reading and writing the English. Evidently she was pleased with my progress because she lent me books and even arranged for her son's tutor to give me some instruction in mathematics.

Some months later I could read a notice on a wall as I went to buy bonnet trimmings. ['What on earth were bonnet trimmings?']

'International Exhibition of Industry, Art and Science'

I asked James what it meant. He told me he would take me to see it and it would be a most thrilling experience. When the time came, my mistress gave us all, in turn, an extra afternoon off to visit the Exhibition. The Meadows were utterly transformed with real buildings, galleries, musical performances and displays of every kind imaginable. If I wrote of all I saw I would be writing yet. All I will say now is, that when I travelled on the electric railway, and saw over three thousand electric lamps illuminating the area, ['Wow, that sounds amazing!'] *I knew that my dear James spoke the truth when he talked of the wonders and the possibilities of science.*

It was a most memorable day, as James had promised. He bought me a mug as a souvenir and afterwards his landlady allowed us to sit with her in her parlour where he showed me his drawings

'Is that all there is?' Gabriella looked up.

'Afraid so.' I said, and explained about the mice.

'Who was James, did you say?'

'James Gabriel was your great-great-grandfather. I told you about him this morning,' I said.

'What did he invent?'

'Lots of things. We've got some of his papers upstairs,' said my mother. 'And do you know what? Whenever he was congratulated on his achievements, apparently he would claim that Chrissie, as he called her, was not only his wife but also his right-hand man. She turned out to have a mind for inventing too.'

'And you're called after him in a way,' I said, keen to reinforce the connection. 'Gabriel. Gabriella.'

She went so far as to smile at me.

'And you're called after her. Christina.' She came and stood next to me. 'I wouldn't really want to leave school at fourteen. I'd miss my friends.' She looked at me, sheepishly for her. 'I think I'd like to be an inventor. Can you do inventing at university?'

'I don't think there's an inventing course,' I said carefully, not wanting to ruin this amicable conversation. 'But you could do engineering or physics and take it from there, maybe?'

'My physics teacher said I was excellent at problem solving. Oh, you said that this morning. And I'm good at drawing. That would be useful for inventing, wouldn't it – Christina?' she added cheekily.

I put my arm round her and squeezed her shoulder. 'Definitely useful, Gabriella.'

She actually hugged me back then looked at my mother.

'And the first Christina really couldn't read or write until this Lady Something taught her?'

Mum nodded. 'When she was about eighteen. Yes. Some people thought that girls shouldn't be educated the way they are now but learn only housekeeping skills. Christina was lucky. Her employer was a very enlightened woman.'

'Housekeeping skills! Bo-ring!' Gabriella scoffed. 'That's discrimination. It's sexist.' She went over and looked down at the paper again. 'She sounds great. And so does he. What drawings do you think he showed her?'

'We'll never know,' my mother said. 'It could be either his Mechanical Dust Eater or his Superior Writing Machine. He was experimenting with those around that time, according to his papers.'

'Can I see them, Granny? I wonder what the mug he bought her was like?'

'We used to keep toothbrushes in it – imagine that, it was antique even then – when I was a little girl but the handle got broken. I've still got it though. Come upstairs and I'll show it to you, and James' drawings.'

'Are you coming, Christina?' my daughter grinned at me. It was an olive branch and I seized it with both hands.

'I'm right behind you, Gabriella,' I said.

'Now,' Mum said, half an hour later when we came downstairs, 'how about we go to the kitchen and make some chocolate brownies? Housekeeping skills are not to be sniffed at either, you know!'

'Cool,' said Christina's great-great-granddaughter – future inventor, cake maker, light bearer for the next generation.

Published in *The People's Friend* under the title *Bright Spark*

The Night the Band Played

I'm remembering the night The Ceilidh Band came to our village hall.

They were to play at the first event to be held in the hall since the war ended. For six years the hall had been used for all sorts of other purposes: first aid classes, soup kitchen, store room for the Home Guard. So this was a big occasion. I was ten and could barely remember a time when there wasn't a war, couldn't remember the amateur dramatics, the concerts and harvest suppers my mother told me about. The Ceilidh Band – that was their name – coming to play for us, followed by tea and cakes, was the most exciting thing that had ever happened as far as I was concerned.

I stood gazing at the announcement in the post office window for the umpteenth time. Dad had taught me to play the fiddle but I looked at that poster and longed for a piano accordion.

'I bet I could play one of them,' I said to Will, pointing to the picture of the burly musician, his fingers stretched over the keys and buttons. 'Do you think he'd let me have a go?'

'You, Alex? You couldn't even lift it.' He felt my upper arm. 'Not with your puny little muscles.'

I forgot about the accordion for the moment as I fell on Will. My muscles might have been puny but they were strong enough to wrestle him to the ground.

Mr MacRae tapped on the post office window.

'Alexandra Fraser. What would your mother say if she saw you scrapping in the street?'

Alexandra! I hated my full name. Will and I picked ourselves up and I said, "Sorry, Mr MacRae' and we went off to our den at the bottom of Will's garden.

'Now, Will,' I said, 'I really want to play that piano accordion and you've got to help me.'

As I spoke, I could picture myself up on stage wearing the Fraser tartan kilt that had been my big brother's, picking

39

up the piano accordion, instantly learning how to play all my favourite tunes, and then listening to the thunderous applause.

'Me? How?' Will burrowed in the earth and picked up a worm. 'I'm sure this is the worm I saw yesterday. He's a beauty.' He stroked his finger along the worm's length.

'They all look the same,' I said. I thought of pointing out to Will that a worm is a she as well as a he, but I had more important things to talk about. 'William!' Will hated his full name too. 'What we could do is this. When the band stops playing to have their tea you distract the accordion player somehow and then I'll have a go of it.'

Will put the worm on the ground and watched it slither away. He wouldn't look me in the eye and said something I couldn't quite hear.

'Don't mumble, boy, can't abide a boy who mumbles', I said, imitating a Sunday School teacher we'd once had and Will looked up and laughed before sticking his chin in his chest and mumbling again. All I could catch was, 'won't be going ... .'

'What? Nonsense.' It was one of my mother's favourite words. 'Of course you're going to the ceilidh. Everyone's going. What d'you mean?'

Mumble, mumble. 'Dad says there'll be dancing and I'll have to dance with you.'

'Well! If that's all. I don't want to dance with you either, Will MacLeod, so you needn't worry about that,' I said. 'But I need your help so of course you're coming; besides, my Auntie Eileen's making a fruit cake and,' I paused for dramatic effect, 'a chocolate cake.'

So then all I needed to do was to work out a plan, and the cake gave me an idea.

The Ceilidh Band was not to be the only entertainment that night; lots of people were doing a turn including me, Alexandra Fraser. My dad and I were to play *Westering Home* and *The Rowan Tree* on the fiddle and he kept me in for the three evenings before, practising over and over. I didn't get a chance to see Will again until we arrived as the ladies were setting out the tables – and The Ceilidh Band were setting up their instruments.

'Will, look! There he is'

Up on the stage a large man in a kilt and velvet jacket was unpacking a lovely shiny red piano accordion. He lifted it carefully onto the floor and put the case out of sight behind the curtain.

Then my mother's voice came from the other end of the hall. 'Al-ex! Wi-ill! Come he-re!'

We looked at each other, shrugged our shoulders and slithered towards her on the newly polished floor.

'We could do with a hand here. There's that much stuff. Will, unpack those rock buns on to that plate, carefully mind. Alex, you do the same with the shortbread. AND NO EATING. You can have your fill at the interval but if I see one crumb on either of you now there'll be BIG TROUBLE.'

By the time we'd finished that, and run round the village borrowing more plates and another tablecloth, Dad had arrived and he made me have another practice in the corridor. Then, as my mother tweaked my white socks, although they were straight already, Mr MacRae announced that Mr Sandy Fraser and Miss Alexandra Fraser were going to start the evening off with two tunes on the fiddle. So the next time I saw the piano accordion was after the other turns, when it was time to push the chairs to the side to make room for the dancing – and for The Ceilidh Band to play.

There was a drum kit and two fiddles and, of course, the shiny red piano accordion. The accordion player lifted the instrument as if it was as light as a feather, wrapping it round himself, balancing it on his knees and flexing his fingers. One of the fiddlers gave the others the nod and they began with *Marie's Wedding*.

I watched as people started dancing. My mother and father and Will's parents and Mr and Mrs MacRae, everybody, all the grown-ups were dancing and looking happy and sort of shiny in their best clothes. I smoothed

41

down my kilt and pulled up my socks and sidled to the stage. I saw the way the accordion went in and out and how fast the musician's fingers had to go, and I tapped my foot in time to the cheerful music. Every tune I played on the fiddle always seemed so sad and far away.

A Dashing White Sergeant came next and I found myself between my parents dancing round and round the hall. Then my father asked if he might have the pleasure of dancing the Gay Gordons with me and after it, as we sat down to catch our breath, Mr MacRae announced that it was the interval.

Will was supposed to go straight over and bring the accordion player down to the table, telling him about the chocolate cake and introducing him to its baker. Auntie Eileen could talk for Scotland, or so my dad always said, so we reckoned he'd not get away from her until the interval was over.

I couldn't see Will anywhere. I peered into the corridor and then I ran all the way round the hall, twice. As I passed the table the second time I could see that the chocolate cake was disappearing fast. Auntie Eileen stopped speaking to Mr MacRae long enough to ask me if I'd like a piece and of course I did and then my mother came up and said I was to stop running around and stay right there until the interval was over.

'Mother, have you seen Will?' I called after her and she turned and said Will had had one of his nosebleeds and he was with his father in the gents' cloakroom trying to stop it with cold water.

So that was that. I stood beside the table eating chocolate cake and I packed away some shortbread and a few rock buns too while I tried to think of another plan. Then I heard Auntie Eileen say, 'That's a great band you have, we're fair enjoying the music,' and I turned to find the accordion player standing right beside me.

'This is my niece, Alex,' Auntie Eileen went on, 'you'll have seen her earlier on stage. She's a grand wee fiddler.'

He looked down and smiled. 'Hello Alex, I'm Finlay. That looked to me like a good fiddle.'

I said, 'It was my big brother Johnny's.'

'Does he not want to play it any more?'

Auntie Eileen leaned across the table and said in a hoarse whisper, 'He didn't come back from the war, poor laddie.'

I never saw my father cry, not even when we got the telegram about Johnny, although maybe he did when no one was looking. But now this big man took out his handkerchief and wiped his eyes.

'My boy, my son David, he never came back either.'

I remembered how, at the end of his last leave, Johnny had carried me on his shoulders into the station and how, when the train was pulling away, he'd stuck his head out of the window and said 'See you soon!' and I'd gone alongside waving until I ran out of platform.

And I started to cry too.

Auntie Eileen came bustling round the table and made Finlay and me sit down and she stirred two spoonfuls of sugar into two cups of tea and stood over us until we'd drunk some and then she had to go back to serving other people.

We sat there, drinking the hot tea, when Will came sliding up. 'Hey, Alex. I had a nosebleed. What about the accordion? Will I do it now?'

I scowled at him and shook my head.

Will took no notice. 'Alex! Do you still want a shot of the accordion?'

Finlay looked at Will and then at me.

I twisted my hanky into a knot.

'Well,' I began.

When I'd finished, Finlay stood up and thanked Auntie Eileen for the tea then he held out his hand to me and we marched down the hall, Will prancing behind.

'I taught David to play,' he said 'and I'll teach you if it's all right with your mum and dad. We'll have a word with them. But first, before the dancing starts again, come and have a wee shot.'

I'm remembering that long-ago night as I leave the top table to take my place in my very own ceilidh band, The

43

Alexandra Sisters. I'm going to do one number with them now and then I have to take to the floor for another reason.

I smile across the room at my new husband. He's still prone to nosebleeds but, as the local vet, he's moved on from keeping pet worms to looking after cows, sheep and horses.

He says I'm not *quite* as bossy as I used to be, and he won't mind at all having to dance the first waltz with me; in fact, he's looking forward to it.

I lift my lovely shiny red piano accordion, smile again at Will, and begin to play.

Published in *The People's Friend*

The New Eighteen

'It's dangerous for a girl to travel on her own,' Ted grumbled to Jess, 'and what do you have to go so far away for? I bet there's loads of places round here you haven't seen.'

'Oh, Ted, leave her be,' I said. He'd been singing the same song ever since Jess first started talking about her gap year.

'Wales, you could go to Wales.' Ted leaned over for another piece of cake. 'Or Scotland. Your Mam and I had a holiday in Scotland once, Loch Lomond – you had a good time there, Annie, didn't you, love?'

Maybe Ted had forgotten but that was our honeymoon. We did have a good time, a lovely time, and it was memorable too because it was one of the few holidays we ever had.

'Yes, Ted, I did,' I replied, 'but our Jess has got other plans.'

Most people seem to go east for a gap year but not Jess. She loved reading about India and Thailand but that's not where she wanted to go.

No, Jess had longed to travel 'out west' ever since she was a little girl and I'd read *Little House on the Prairie* to her. She called us Maw and Paw for a whole summer and pretended the garden shed was a covered wagon, and she persuaded us to let her and a friend sleep out in it one night. When we moved on to *Anne of Green Gables* she wanted to go to Prince Edward Island to see the maple trees and red roads and shining lakes for herself.

I wished so much then that we could take her to far-flung places but Ted was just starting up his business. Money was tight and anyway Ted would never take that sort of time off. So Jess, a dreamy child like her heroine Anne, kept reading, and saw the world in her imagination.

Funny how things turn out.

Ted sold the garage – got a tidy price for it and all – and gave Jess some money, and a gap year turned from a dream into a possibility. The journeys she'd taken in her mind came back to her, and then she thought of all the other books she'd loved since. She spent months surfing the internet and looking at maps and guide books, and she worked out a trip that started in Prince Edward Island, crossed to the west of Canada, came down through California and ended two months later in New York, visiting the settings of favourite books all along the way.

Ted – never a reader himself – was determined to throw cold water on the scheme.

'"A gap year,"' he scoffed. 'When your mam and I were young there was no such thing.'

I wanted to tell him not to tread on her dreams but I knew his heart was in the right place. Although Jess was a big girl now, she'd always be his baby.

'It's not really a gap *year*, Dad,' Jess said, 'it's a gap two months. None of my friends can come, not for that length of time. I'll be fine on my own. I'll email you and Mam as often as I can, every day probably. I've worked out what I want to do and I'm going to the travel agents tomorrow to talk it over with them and book the first few flights. Mam thinks I'm doing the right thing, don't you, Mam?'

'You deserve it, love' I said, 'we'll miss you of course, but I know you'll have a wonderful time. It's been as good as going myself hearing your plans and seeing how happy you are.'

'I'd be a darn sight happier if you weren't going on your own,' Ted growled.

'Dad, for goodness sake …' Jess started, but then she put down her cup and looked at me.

'Mam! Why don't you come with me?'

'Don't be daft,' I said.

'Why not? Oh Mam, imagine it. Why didn't I think of it before? If it hadn't been for you reading me bedtime stories ... and it's not as if I'm backpacking and staying in crummy

46

hostels. It will be trains and buses and inns and motels. I'd love us to do it together.'

'But what about your dad?'

'Well, it was practically his idea – wasn't it, Dad? He'll be all right. Auntie May's next door to keep an eye out and the twins will pop in – and we'll teach him how to cook and use the email.'

Ted spluttered into his tea.

'Oh, please say you'll come, Mam,' Jess begged. I couldn't resist her.

Yes, it's funny how things turn out.

When Ted had given Jess that money he thought she would do something 'sensible' with it but here he was, one sunny July morning – carrying my new suitcase and asking me for the hundredth time if I was sure I had my passport – waving his daughter, and his wife, off on the first leg of their journey to Green Gables, a flight to Halifax, Nova Scotia, Canada.

Jess's twins were there too, promising they'd help Auntie May keep an eye on their granddad.

I was looking forward to seeing the places we'd curled up and read about together, but most of all I was looking forward to spending time with my daughter. Jess married at twenty but her husband died when their twins were just babies. Books were her lifeline, her escape, as they had always been.

But now the girls were independent and, with unpaid leave from work, Jess could actually go where her imagination had taken her, go on what her twins were calling 'Mum's gap year'.

Now it was Gran's gap year too.

'Forty-two is the new eighteen, Mum!' said one of the girls, as she hugged Jess goodbye.

'What about sixty-three, Annie?' Ted asked me, 'is that the new anything?'

He was taking the whole thing pretty well, considering. I swatted him with my newspaper.

'I'm eighteen as well,' I said.

Because just then, inside, I didn't feel a day older.

Published in *The People's Friend* under the title *Travelling Hopefully*

New Tricks, Old Tricks

caNyuc Omefor jtnchs un! gpanx

Meg peered at the tiny screen. It would need the Enigma machine to decipher it, she thought, but it had taken her half an hour to get this far and she didn't know how to delete her mistakes. It would just have to do.

Luckily, since she was replying to Rosie's text, she didn't have to find her number, just press 'send'.

Rosie's message to her, although not in what you would call English, was somehow comprehensible:

How r u? c u soon? Rxxx

She hoped that her granddaughter would understand that she was invited for lunch on Sunday. It would be lovely to see Rosie and it would mean that she could tell Drina, Rosie's mother, that Rosie had had at least one decent meal that week. It was only because Meg lived a bus ride away from where Rosie was studying fashion design that Drina had agreed to her daughter moving to London at all. Really, she would have liked Rosie to have gone and lived with Meg and it had taken tact on everyone's part to point out how more practical it was for Rosie to live in the self-catering flats belonging to the college.

There was a little whirring noise which meant she'd got a reply and that Rosie had understood the invitation.

Thanx Gran. Cn I brng my friend Jean?

That was easy to reply to.

Yes.

She would have liked to add: *That will be lovely, hope Jean's not a vegetarian; is she one of your flatmates? I thought they were called Gemma and Fariah. Have you been in touch with your mum and has she been practising her texting? Can I ask you while you're here to change a light bulb I can't reach, and maybe take some papers to the recycling bank?* But that would have taken at least an hour, would no doubt look like gibberish and, besides, she could say it all when she saw Rosie, so she added a kiss and sent the brief reply off into the ether.

'Mmm, that smells so good,' exclaimed Rosie when Meg opened the door on Sunday. 'Gran does a fab roast chicken,' she added turning to her companion. 'Gran, this is Jean; he's in my class. Jean, this is my gran.'

To her surprise, Meg saw a young man standing beside Rosie but the mystery was solved when he held out his hand.

'Rosie has told me so much about you,' he said in a soft French accent. 'Thank you for asking me to lunch, Madame … '

'Please call me Meg. Do come in both of you. My late husband, Rosie's grandpa, and I had several happy holidays in France, Jean. But I'm glad you speak such good English because my French is very rusty. Now, please sit here and I'll fetch the sherry. Rosie, could you give me a hand in the kitchen?'

'Do you like him, Gran?' whispered Rosie as she reached up to the top shelf for Meg's best dinner-set.

'He seems charming. And he's doing fashion design too?'

'He's brilliant. The next Yves St Laurent, I think. He found this material for me in a charity shop; I just finished making it up last night.'

She twirled round to show off her dress, floral glazed cotton with a sweetheart neckline.

'And he's gorgeous too, don't you think?'

'Very handsome. Are you – as they say – an item?'

Rosie blushed. 'Well, I hope so. Early days. I wanted you to meet him before I say anything to Mum.'

'I'm to pave the way, am I? You know, when you think she's being over-protective it's because you're her one and only and she hasn't come to terms with you being all grown-up.'

'I know, Gran, I know. OK, what else are we having for lunch? Your special? Oh, *brill*. Jean,' she called out, 'Gran's ultra famous and fabulous white chocolate mousse cake is on the menu today.'

Meg chuckled to herself. Drina wasn't entirely wrong when she said Rosie was still her little girl.

She got the sherry out of the fridge and put it with glasses on a tray and Rosie held the door open for her.

Jean hadn't sat down where Meg had indicated. Instead he was standing by the sofa, turning one of the cushions round and round in his hands.

'Did you make this, Meg?'

'Yes, I did,' Meg said. 'Years ago now. Why?'

'I see where Rosie gets her clever use of colour from. These are very stylish.'

'Are they?' Rosie sounded unflatteringly surprised. 'They're just Gran's old cushions. They've always been on that sofa.'

Jean's dark eyes met Meg's. 'They are made from crochet, are they not? See all the different stitches, Rosie. They are very, very – how do you say it – intricot.'

'Intricate. So they are. I've never really looked at them before. They're ancient though. Wait a minute. They're vintage!' Rosie looked at the cushions with new respect.

Meg laughed. 'Why don't the pair of you sit down on these vintage cushions and I'll pour you a glass of sherry.'

At the end of the meal when even Rosie couldn't manage any more cake Meg started to clear the table.

'I'll make some coffee.'

Jean jumped up. 'Please let me help you. I'm very good at washing up.'

'Bless you,' said Meg, 'but I have a dishwasher. If you could help carry them through I'll load it up and then we can have some coffee.'

'And I'll give you lesson number seven hundred and fifty on texting, Gran,' teased Rosie. 'Mum's better at it than you now. Just.'

'It's hard to teach old dogs new tricks and I'm a very old dog. Rosie dear, could you change my bedroom light? I can't reach it and the doctor said I wasn't to stand on chairs. There are bulbs in the hall cupboard.'

Meg and Jean tidied away the lunch dishes and Jean made the coffee. What a delightful young man he was. Even Drina would surely think so too. Who knew what would happen in the future, whether Rosie and Jean would settle down together or not. As Rosie had said herself, it was early days. But it would be nice. Visits to France, half-French great-grandchildren …

Meg's reverie was interrupted by Rosie coming back into the room in a positive sunburst of colour.

'Gran, hope you don't mind. I found all this wool in the cupboard. Mum always says you never throw anything out.'

'I did try to teach you to knit when you were little but you were always more interested in sewing, Rosie.'

Jean examined the wool seriously. Then he looked up. 'I would be interested to learn, Meg. If you would like to teach me. To knit, but first please to crochet.'

'You want to make cushions?' Rosie raised her eyebrows in disbelief.

'Oh no. Scarves. Belts. Even dresses. In very fine wool. Like cobwebs.'

'Goodness. Yes, I'd be happy to,' Meg said. 'Shall we start today?'

'Jean, you're the new dog who's going to learn old tricks,' Rosie laughed.

Meg went to look for her crochet hooks.

It was good to know there was life in the old dog yet.

Published in *The People's Friend*

Bicycles for Two

Every day on our way home from school June and I stopped by the bicycle shop to press our noses against its window. We linked our pinky fingers and made a wish as we gazed at two shiny new bikes that looked just the right size for us.

June had got a scholarship to the Grammar School the year after I did. At least now I had someone to walk with but it was much further away than our primary school, there was no direct bus, and however fast we went we were always late.

'Isabel, June, what can we do about this?' Dad asked, rather helplessly, when we took home a letter from the Head complaining that we had missed Assembly every morning that week.

'We-ll,' said June, for the dozenth time, 'if we had bicycles we could get to school much faster. Could they be our Christmas presents?'

Dad shook his head.

'Can't manage them this year,' he said, for the dozenth time, 'what with all the uniform and books and sports stuff you girls need for school. Your mum and me are proud of you getting scholarships, you know that, but I can't rise to bicycles I'm afraid.'

Mum was always busy with our new baby brother, David, who was rather delicate. We didn't want to bother her about bicycles but we mentioned it to the aunts after school one day.

Dad's aunts, Aunt Ann and Aunt Edie, lived round the corner from us, and since David's arrival we often went to their house for tea. They had lived together for twenty years, ever since Aunt Edie's husband was killed in the Blitz.

Aunt Edie opened the door. 'Aunt Ann's made a very nice shepherd's pie,' she said, 'with melted cheese on top. It'll be ready in a jiffy. Have a glass of milk and tell us what you've been doing today.'

June threw herself into a chair by the fire and lifted Mittens from the rug to sit on her knee.

'We're in trouble with the Head because we were late again,' she grumbled. 'It's such a long walk. And of course Dad's work is in the opposite direction so he can't drive us. If we had bikes we could be there in ten minutes probably. We've seen these fab red ones in the shop in the high street.'

'Red bicycles! Whatever next!' said Aunt Edie. 'Could you maybe try and leave a bit earlier? Or sort out your books the night before?'

I said, 'We do, but we have to get our breakfast, and Dad's, and do the washing-up and make our beds to help Mum and it takes ages.'

'Have you said all this to your father?' Aunt Ann started to dish out the shepherd's pie.

'Yes,' said June sadly, 'but he says he can't afford bikes this Christmas.'

'He's worried about things at work at the moment. Don't trouble him just now, dears.' Aunt Ann went to the sideboard and brought out a photograph album. 'Did you know your Aunt Edie and I used to love cycling?'

She brought the album over to the table. 'Look, that's us, up near Loch Lomond, wouldn't you say, Edie?'

Aunt Edie put her spectacles on.

'You're right, Ann, it is. The Ladies' Bicycle Club's summer outing, 1933.'

June and I stared at the Ladies. They all had short hair and wore baggy shorts and patterned jumpers and knee-length socks.

'You cycled to Loch Lomond! That's miles! Which ones are you?' I asked. Looking at Aunt Ann and Aunt Edie now, in their pleated skirts, lace-up shoes, and greyish hair in knots at the back of their necks, I found it hard to believe that any of them could be.

Aunt Edie pointed to the two fair-haired girls at the end of the row, laughing and holding on to their bicycles.

'That's us, there. And that's, oh what was her name, Ann?'

While June and I tucked into shepherd's pie the aunts remembered every detail about everyone in the photograph, every outing they'd ever been on with the Ladies' Bicycle Club and agreed that in the summers when they were young every day was gloriously sunny.

June rolled her eyes at me and we smiled at each other. The aunts' bicycles – 'bikes' wasn't a grand enough word for them – were tall and stately looking, with baskets on the front. Very old-fashioned. You certainly wouldn't describe them as 'fab', not like those red bikes in the shop window, really up-to-date and expensive-looking with racing handlebars and white saddlebags.

I imagined packing my saddlebag with my books and gym kit and cycling off to school, my hockey stick tucked under my arm. Parking the bike and strolling into class instead of dashing in like a breathless beetroot knowing I was going to be in trouble.

'Do you still cycle, Aunt Edie?' I asked

'Goodness, no. Haven't done for years. Whatever happened to those bicycles, Ann? They didn't come with us to this house.'

'Probably mouldering in George's garage,' Aunt Ann replied. 'Our brother never throws anything out as you know. Edie, those shorts! Those socks! What did we look like?'

Eventually Aunt Edie put the album away.

'That was a grand trip down memory lane,' she said. 'Now girls, I'm on pudding duty tonight.' She spooned tinned pears, our favourite, into two bowls and poured Carnation milk over them.

We changed the subject to Saturday's hockey match.

It was four weeks later, Christmas Eve, and we were looking forward to Granny, our mother's mother, coming to stay with us.

June and I went down town to get out library books for holiday reading. On the way home we looked longingly in the bike shop window as usual.

The red bicycles were gone.

We looked at each other, hardly daring to speak.

'Do you think Dad ... ?' I said, at the same time as June said, 'Maybe the aunts ... ?'

Aunt Ann and Aunt Edie always did their Christmas shopping separately.

Aunt Edie loved the department store, especially what she called the 'smellies' section. She bought us pink or blue bubble bath in plastic bottles shaped like poodles or snowmen, or tins of talcum powder, or soap that looked and smelled exactly like lemons. She bought new wrapping paper every year, bright with robins and Santas, and she bought real ribbon from the haberdashery department to tie up her parcels.

Aunt Ann used paper that people had wrapped her own presents in the year before, and she tied them with string. From her we got pencil cases, the kind with a pencil, a propelling pencil, a rubber, and a pen for dipping into ink – although we never did; books by classic authors; tapestry kits with pictures of kittens or puppies.

So it didn't seem very likely that they would buy us bicycles. 'I doubt it,' I said gloomily. 'Some other lucky girls will be getting them for Christmas.' I couldn't help feeling a spark of hope though.

But all thought of bikes went from our heads when we turned the corner and saw Mum standing by our neighbour's car with David in her arms.

'Girls, Granny's neighbour's phoned to say she fell over in the garden. They think she's broken her leg. Jack's kindly giving me a lift to the station and I've phoned your Dad. He'll come up to Granny's after work. Go round to the aunts, I've told them what's happening.'

'Poor Granny! But what about Christmas?' I asked.

'I don't know, Isabel. I might have to stay to look after Granny and who knows how icy the roads are will be. Be good girls. We'll let you know what's happening as soon as we can.'

I pulled back the shawl so that we could see David, all cosily wrapped up in the bunny pram suit Granny had knitted for him, and a hat with a pom-pom. He gave a kick and a gummy smile when he saw us. We each put a finger into his little hands and he gripped on. I was sad to think that we might not be spending his first Christmas together.

We watched the car turn the corner on the way to the station and then made our way round to the aunts. They were both waiting at the door. They hugged us which they never usually did.

'It's Christmas Day tomorrow!' said Aunt Edie. 'Thank goodness you two are here. We've so much to do.'

Over the next few hours we made mince pies, helped to clean and dust, admired the dumpling Aunt Ann had made months before and kept wrapped in a cloth in the larder, and the fruit cake which Aunt Edie had covered with thick white icing and silver balls. We set a little tree in a pot in the window bay and decorated it with glass ornaments, and June made a star out of tinsel for the top.

Just after tea the phone went, making us jump. It was Dad, ringing from a kiosk.

'Granny's leg's in plaster. She's fine, but she'll have to spend Christmas in hospital. She sends her love,' he said. 'It's snowing up here – some of the roads are blocked. We're going to try and come home but we might have to turn back and stay at Granny's house. We can't risk getting stuck somewhere with David in the car.'

'Right,' said Aunt Ann. 'It's going to be a long night. Goodness knows when your Mum and Dad will turn up but we must be ready. We'll make some sandwiches and sausage rolls and set a tray.'

She found some music on the wireless and we worked in time to it, dancing round the kitchen, making kilts out of dishcloths, and cutting funny shapes out of leftover pastry.

Then it was nine o'clock, our usual bedtime. 'Please can we stay up,' I begged, 'I'm sure we couldn't sleep anyway.'

Aunt Edie got out a compendium of games and we played Snap and Happy Families for a bit.

'Oh,' said June, suddenly, putting her hand of cards down. 'We never took a pair of Dad's long socks with us. We always hang them up by the fire on Christmas Eve. We were going to do one for David too. How will Santa know where to find us?' She looked ready to cry.

I had my suspicions about Santa Claus but I kept them to myself.

Aunt Ann and Aunt Edie looked at each other.

'Maybe we'll give you our presents now,' said Aunt Ann. 'How about that? It would take our minds off things.'

We cheered up and waited for the aunts to go and get parcels but instead Aunt Edie said:

'You'll have to come out to the shed. That's where they are.'

June and I exchanged meaningful glances. My heart was thumping and all I could think about was the space in that shop window where two red bikes with racing handlebars and white saddlebags had been.

'Goodness,' said Aunt Ann as she opened the front door, 'it's snowing. It's going to be a white Christmas.'

We ran across the garden to the shed.

'We didn't like the thought of you being late for school and getting into trouble,' Aunt Ann said, as she flashed her torch over two scarlet bicycles.

Two *stately* scarlet bicycles.

'We rang your Uncle George the night we showed you the photograph album. He said, yes, our bicycles were still in his garage. We bought two new baskets as our presents and George did all the cleaning and repairing then he brought them over in his van. They look as good as they did when we had them,' said Aunt Edie proudly.

'And Edie went too far as usual and asked George to paint them red.' Aunt Ann smiled and shrugged her shoulders. 'They're a sight for sore eyes, so they are.'

Not daring to look at each other, June and I moved forwards to see them close up – the bicycles ridden by two members of the Ladies' Bicycle Club all those years ago. There was a red bow attached to each one and a gift tag with our names on saying, *Hope you have as much fun with these as we did. Love from Aunt Ann and Aunt Edie and Uncle George.*

June sat on her bicycle. It was just the right size. So was mine. I sat up straight and pretended I was wearing baggy shorts and cycling to Loch Lomond. Maybe June and I could try and cycle there too, in the summer. Nobody else we knew had bicycles like these. They were historical! And they were red! And the baskets would hold all our school stuff and any shopping we had to do on the way home.

'I can't wait to go on mine out properly, on the road,' I said.

I got off and rushed over to the aunts. 'The bikes are super-fab, thank you, thank you,' I said, hugging them.

'Oh, get away with you,' said Aunt Ann, but she hugged me back and then June came forward for her turn.

'I'm afraid you can't try them now and maybe not tomorrow if the roads are bad,' said Aunt Edie, 'but never mind, it's something to look forward to. Now, how about a cup of cocoa before bed?'

As we went back in we saw car lights coming down the road.

We stood there, Aunt Ann, Aunt Edie, June and me, hoping and hoping that it was Mum and Dad and David.

The car came to a stop outside the aunts' house. Mum opened the passenger door and held out her arms and we ran into them.

Dad got out and came round to us.

'Granny will get out of hospital in a few days,' said Mum. 'We'll go up and take her back here for New Year.'

'Very good news,' said Aunt Edie.

June tugged at Dad's arm.

'We've got bikes! Bright red bikes!'

Dad put his hand up to brush the snow from his face before he reached into the back seat for David's carrycot.

'Bikes? How? Who … ?'

'June! You can tell him later. What in the world are we doing standing around out here in the cold?' Aunt Ann said briskly. 'Come away in to the fire. Now, give me your coats and sit here,' she commanded Dad and Mum. 'Isabel, the wee pet's asleep. Take the carrycot upstairs. June, help Aunt Edie in the kitchen. Take through those sandwiches you made, and the cups and saucers.'

While Mum and Dad were eating and drinking and getting warm June and I sprawled at the table with our cocoa, trying not to yawn or draw attention to ourselves.

I thought of Granny safely tucked up in hospital. I thought of baby David and how when he was bigger and stronger we could give him rides on our very own bicycles, even teach him to cycle by himself.

Through half-closed eyes I saw Mum and Dad sitting on the sofa in front of the fire and I saw Aunt Ann and Aunt Edie pouring tea, bringing through hot sausage rolls, getting more coal. I saw the tree, its decorations glittering in the yellow light of the standard lamp. The curtains weren't drawn and the snow was piling up on the window-sill.

'That was grand,' said Dad, putting his plate on the floor. 'That went down a treat.'

'I think we'll all have a piece of my cake,' said Aunt Edie, nodding at Aunt Ann and looking significantly at the mantelpiece.

I followed her gaze and looked at the clock. The small hand was on twelve and the big hand had just crept past it.

'It's Christmas Day!' I said.

'I haven't wrapped any presents,' said Mum, 'And I forgot to tell you to pick up the goose from the butcher's. I'm sorry, girls, it's a funny sort of Christmas this year.'

'We don't mind, we've got our bikes!' said June. We went over and wriggled in between Dad and Mum on the sofa.

'Guess what!' I said. 'We won't be late for school any more. And in the summer we're going on a long bike ride like Aunt Ann and Aunt Edie did.'

As it turned out, a few months later Dad's work transferred him down south. Our school was round the corner from our new house – we could start walking five minutes before the bell and still get there on time. But at the weekends out came the bicycles for rides around the country park with our new friends.

Eventually and inevitably – they had been thirty years old and counting when we got them – they were beyond repair and disposed of.

Nowadays everyone is keen on getting fit, and cycling is very popular again. There is always someone in our growing families – mine, June's and David's – who is taking it up, whether on a tricycle or mountain bike or, yes, asking Santa to bring them the latest model.

For years we three siblings have hosted Christmas year and year about. It's always a wonderful day with us all, and Mum and Dad, still hale in their eighties.

And guess what June and I are getting this year …

Our daughters have decided that their mums should get more exercise and they've clubbed together with their dads to give us each a bicycle.

They say you never forget how to ride a bike. I'm hoping that's true.

And on Christmas morning June and I will remember that snowy night and the scarlet bicycles and the dear aunts who gave them to us. We'll bring out the old photograph album and look at Aunt Ann and Aunt Edie in their shorts and patterned jumpers and, who knows, maybe one day we will cycle in their memory all the way to Loch Lomond.

Published in *The People's Friend*

Seeing Natalie

'I am a hologram,' thought Marty, blinking in front of the bathroom mirror without his glasses on. 'Now you see me, now you don't.'

His ex-wife thought he was a hologram, like the one of Frankenstein's monster in the World of Illusions he'd taken their daughter to last week. He was invisible to her most of the time until she took the trouble to move and get a different view. And then she didn't like what she saw.

Not for the first time, Irene had just phoned to cancel Natalie's visit two hours before he was due to pick her up, this time citing an overlooked birthday party invitation and an incipient cold. He would have believed one or the other but not both, and the only consolation was that he was certain that this must be to fit in with a change of plan for Irene and was not Natalie's own wish. Or perhaps Irene was punishing him. Last week he had told her, out of Natalie's hearing, that he was seeing someone, his first serious relationship since the divorce. She hadn't asked any questions, not even Suzanne's name, but pursed up her lips in a very Irene sort of way.

So, if Nat has a cold, she can't go to the party, he said, unable to stop himself sounding sarcastic.

Irene pretended not to hear and said, about next weekend – could he please not take her to that burger place again, didn't he know how many preservatives they used, an American scientist had left a hamburger in its bun out on his lab table for six months and nothing had happened to it, it looked and smelt exactly the same, even the flies ignored it.

He opened and shut his mouth several times during this speech and eventually just pressed the disconnect button. Once – once – about six months ago now, he had taken Natalie to 'that burger place', dashing into the nearest restaurant to get out of a thunderstorm.

He would call back later to speak to Natalie but now he should phone to cancel the pottery painting session he'd booked for her this afternoon. She'd been looking forward to it. That was to have been followed by a visit to the play park and then back to the flat where he had the ingredients for making lasagne. He imagined Natalie helping to chop and stir and assemble. No one, well, not even Irene, could accuse him of not being hands-on, even if he was just a hologram dad. Now you see me, now you don't.

Now thirty-six lonely hours stretched ahead of him. Suzanne was away for the weekend visiting her parents. He supposed he could read the pile of documents his new office had sent him but they held no appeal, not when he'd been psyched up to hold Natalie's hand and listen to her seven-year-old chatter, to entertain her and to watch her fall asleep cuddling the rabbit that kept her bed warm when she wasn't here. Making lasagne for one was too sad even to contemplate.

He leaned forward and squinted. Maybe those lines on his forehead, those dark shadows under his eyes, were just an illusion, and really he was twenty-five, smooth skinned and bright-eyed with his arm around Irene – no, not Irene, not even in his memories – his arm around a beautiful Italian girl at the top of the Visite dal Tetto near where they'd spent their honeymoon. He remembered the panorama of the town from the rooftop, sunlit, full of promise.

But if it had been a beautiful Italian girl and not Irene, there wouldn't be Natalie.

Her favourite thing last week had been what looked like a bowl of liquorice allsorts but when you reached out for one there was only space. Natalie hadn't been disappointed – she didn't like liquorice allsorts – but had spent ages letting the phantom sweets spill from one hand to the other.

Marty had gone to look at a set of mirrors. One showed the self you were used to seeing when you looked in the mirror. The other showed you as others saw you – not the same face he was discomfited and rather horrified to find. Why had no one told him that his mouth had a funny twist to the left and that his hair seemed to be receding more on one side than the other?

When Natalie came over she peered solemnly into each mirror and said that she looked exactly the same in both of them, silly daddy. Marty flipped her fair ponytail and laughed, but he realised with a surge of joy that her pink smile quirked up ever so slightly to the left, and he saw afresh that the hazel eyes flecked with green were his, and his father's before him. Natalie had Irene's retroussé nose and small ears flat against the side of her head, and if he was honest these features were an improvement on what he might have handed down.

What were the chances of her coming into being, of that sperm meeting that egg and latching on to it? Of his little girl growing to life as perfect as she was, not just a medley of Marty and Irene but of the generations that had gone before, plus something that was her very own? One in a million or more. What if the egg had evaded the marauding sperm and both had floated on into oblivion? No Natalie. It didn't bear thinking about.

There were hundreds of Natalies and Martys in wall of mirror balls in the next gallery. I've got loads of sisters just like me, Natalie said excitedly, as the mirrors turned and twinkled starry faces towards them, and Marty wondered if she ever minded that she didn't even have one real sister, nor a brother.

Not yet anyway.

His relationship with Suzanne was just passed the fledgling stage. He knew that she would like to have children but they hadn't yet discussed having them together. She would make a wonderful mother, so warm and calm and straightforward. His life was so much better since he met her. Made redundant, ironically, from the job whose long hours had been the last straw that drove Irene away, he had, with Suzanne's encouragement, applied for a new one he'd thought outside his capabilities. And he got it, was due to start next month.

He straightened up now, put on his glasses, and grinned. This mirror told the truth. He was no hologram. He saw in front of him the new Business Development Manager for a successful IT company. He saw Natalie's father and Suzanne's boyfriend.

The time was right to introduce his two special girls to each other.

He would go to the pottery place himself this afternoon and paint a mug for his daughter. Pale green, he thought, with stars and a big pink N.

N for Natalie. And N for Next Weekend.

Published in *Woman's Weekly*

Three's a Crowd

My big sister Jane swished into the kitchen wearing her best broderie anglaise blouse and wide red skirt.

'Bob's asked me to go for a walk with him,' she announced to Mum and Pamela and me.

'I thought something like this was going to happen,' said Mum, standing up, 'and where to, might I ask?'

'Just along the riverbank.' Jane headed for the front door and the three of us followed her. Through the frosted glass pane I could see Bob coming up the path. He'd recently moved into our street and when he arrived home from work at exactly the same time as Jane – which seemed to happen rather a lot – they would stand talking at our gate for ages before Mum would knock at the window and shout to Jane that tea was ready.

Now Mum grabbed my school coat off the row of pegs in the hall and bundled my arms into the sleeves. 'You could do with some fresh air. Go with them.'

'Mum!' Jane protested, but Bob rang the bell and Mum almost shoved me from behind so that I tumbled out of the door and down the step.

'Whoa there,' Bob said cheerily, putting out his arm to steady me. 'Hello, I'm Bob.'

'This is my mum and this is my twin sister, Pamela. And this,' said Jane, glaring at me, 'is Toots. She's coming with us.'

Mum pulled me back and whispered in my ear. 'Stick with them, Toots, and don't let them hold hands.' How was I supposed to do that?

The pavement wasn't wide enough for the three of us so I had to walk behind them. Jane turned round every so often to give me the evil eye.

'Do you know what a gooseberry is?'

Of course I knew what a gooseberry was. Yuk. Why was she asking?

Bob turned round sometimes too but he smiled in a friendly way and once he winked at me.

The path by the river was very interesting. I kept stopping to peer into the bushes to see if I could see any birds and to listen to their songs.

Then, up ahead of me, Jane and Bob stopped and I didn't think they were bird watching. I ran to catch up, before they got round to hand-holding, and just when I got to them I slipped and fell right into the river.

It was lucky I had my coat on because it sort of spread out and kept me afloat until Bob jumped in and rescued me. Well, the water wasn't very deep and I might not have actually drowned but I was wet up to my neck, and Bob was wet up to his waist, and Jane was mortified, she said, as we dripped our way home.

'What on earth were you doing?' she asked, and I mumbled something about birds and Bob said he had a good book that would help me identify them and he would pop it through our letterbox for me.

The next time he and Jane were chatting at the gate Mum opened the door instead of knocking at the window. She asked Bob if he would like to come in and have his tea with us. I think she was very impressed that he was a hero and had saved her youngest daughter from a watery grave.

He helped me with my jigsaw while Jane kept hinting that I could do something else, somewhere else, but Mum had told me to stay in the living-room with them while she was making macaroni cheese.

'Gooseberry,' Jane whispered as we went through to the kitchen to eat. But we didn't have gooseberries. We had jam roly-poly and custard.

Bob had tea with us quite often after that and one night as he was leaving he asked Jane to go to the cinema with him on Saturday afternoon.

I knew what was coming.

Mum gave me one of her looks as the three of us left the house. Chin down, eyebrows raised. Her be-sure-you-remember look.

I gave her the thumbs up without Jane or Bob seeing me. Then I turned quickly and grabbed Bob's right hand and Jane's left and swung them back and fore.

'You're too big to do that.' Jane tried to shake my hand off.

'I'm only nine,' I said, making my voice as teeny-tiny as possible.

'But I suppose you're old enough to come out to see *Father of the Bride* with us?'

'I'm old enough to see the film but young enough to swing,' I said, and I tried to lift my feet off the ground. It wasn't a success.

Bob gasped as he tried to keep us all from falling flat on our faces. 'Sure you wouldn't like to go home and we could take you to the park after we've seen the film, Toots?' he asked, when he got his breath back.

'Quite sure, thank you.' I glanced up at him. Actually, I would have liked to go to the park rather than sit in a stuffy old cinema. But Mum promised me a whole banana if I was sitting in between them when the cinema lights went down.

We didn't have bananas very often and when we did Mum cut one in slices and we ate it from bowls with some condensed milk on top – just the one between me, Jane and Pamela. I'd never ever had a whole one all to myself.

Jane and Pamela remember eating bananas before the war but I was born in 1941. I don't remember before the war. I don't remember our dad either. All I know is that the war was a place he went to when I was a baby. He didn't come back and Mum still misses him.

I'd heard her talking to my auntie.

'It's hard being mother *and* father, especially now Jane and Pamela are at that age. Wanting to go out with boys. Their dad would have known what to do.'

'Jane's eighteen and Bob sounds like a nice young man,' Auntie said.

'Well, yes, but you never know,' Mum replied. 'I'm trying not to leave them on their own.'

68

What she meant was that I, Toots, didn't leave them on their own and Jane was fed up with me.

In the cinema I slipped past Bob to follow her along the row of seats.

She looked very, very annoyed. 'Do you know what a gooseberry is?'

There she was, on about gooseberries again.

''course I do. We've got a bush in the garden.' I don't like them. The berries are sour little green bullets. My face puckered up just thinking about them.

Jane shook her head. 'Not that kind. You're being a gooseberry right now,' she said. 'It means that you're tagging along with a couple, with Bob and me. You're the odd one out.'

That explained this gooseberry business but the thought that I was 'the odd one out' made my face pucker up again.

Bob produced a cake of Fry's chocolate cream from his pocket and passed it across to Jane. Their hands touched for a moment but there was nothing I could do about it.

Jane broke the chocolate cream into bits. She passed them to Bob who indicated to me to go first. Jane sighed but drew her hand back and I picked up a piece. I let it melt on my tongue. It was loveliest thing I'd ever tasted.

'Swap places with me,' Jane hissed. 'Please. I'll give you the last piece of chocolate.'

I was tempted, very tempted, but I'd promised Mum. Anyway, just at that moment the lights went down.

The film was funnier than I thought it would be but it was sad too. A man didn't think his daughter was old enough to get married and when she wouldn't change her mind he worried the wedding was going to cost too much. I turned to look at Jane to see if she was enjoying it. She had her head on one side gazing at Bob and Bob was gazing back. Daughters, fathers, weddings. We didn't have a father anymore but I was pretty sure that a wedding and a daughter was what they were thinking about – and it was nothing to do with Spencer Tracy and Elizabeth Taylor.

And I was thinking that I liked Bob, with his Fry's chocolate cream, and his help with jigsaws, and his bird book, and his bravery, and that it would be nice to have a big brother in the family.

It was too late to swap places without make a fuss but when the film finished I pretended that I had to tie my shoelaces and I bent down for much longer than I needed to. There was a kissing noise above my head. Then I skipped behind Jane and Bob as they held hands all the way home.

Not even me tagging along, being a gooseberry, could keep them apart. They were meant to be together.

Mum snorted when I told her that later, when I confessed I hadn't earned my banana.

'You're too young to go to those silly films,' she said. I didn't want to go in the first place so I thought that was very unfair.

Maybe Mum thought so too because she gave me my banana anyway.

That was six months ago. Next week Pamela and I are going to be Jane's bridesmaids when she marries Bob. Mum says Jane is far too young but Bob is very sensible, she always thought so, and she knows he'll make a good husband.

She's not sure though about this lad that's been hanging around our Pamela …

I shook my head very firmly. I wasn't going to be a gooseberry again, not for a whole bunch of bananas.

Published in *The People's Friend*

Acknowledgements

I am grateful to *The People's Friend, Woman's Weekly* and *Woman's Day* for publishing these stories initially.

Many thanks to Mark Blackadder for the cover design.

Five of these stories had their gestation in the Writers' Room at the Southside Centre, to whom I am indebted for ongoing inspiration and camaraderie; I'm indebted for the same reasons to Edinburgh Writers' Club. And I owe so much to the late Gabrielle Green – without her encouragement my stories would still be stuck in my head.

About the author

Kate Blackadder lives in Edinburgh. She has had over forty short stories published in *The People's Friend, Woman's Weekly, The Weekly News* and *Writers' Forum*. In 2008 she won the Muriel Spark Short Story Prize, judged by Maggie O'Farrell. Other stories have been in *New Writing Scotland, Writers' Forum* and long/short-listed for the Jane Austen Award and the Scotsman/Orange Prize.

She also writes serials for *The People's Friend*. The first two, *The Family at Farrshore* and *The Ferryboat,* are now available in large-print editions from libraries, and will soon (2016) be available on Kindle/in print (see synopses below). She has been the guest author at *People's Friend* workshops.

Find out more: http://katewritesandreads.blogspot.co.uk/

The Family at Farrshore

Cathryn is delighted to join an archaeological dig at Farrshore, in the Scottish Highlands. Apart from her professional interest, it means she'll be at a distance from her recently ex-boyfriend, Daniel. Canadian Magnus Macaskill is in Farrshore for his own reasons, one of which is to trace his ancestry. As they spend the summer lodging with the MacLeod family, Cathryn and Magnus are drawn into the small community and to each other. But how will Cathryn react when Daniel reappears in her life?

The Ferryboat

When Judy and Tom Jeffreys are asked by their daughter Holly and her Scottish chef husband Corin if they will join them in buying The Ferryboat hotel in the West Highlands, they take the plunge and move north. The rundown hotel needs much expensive upgrading – and what with local opposition to some of their plans, and worrying about their younger daughter, left down south with her flighty grandma, Judy begins to wonder if they've made a terrible mistake.